CAN YOU DISCOVER AN ALIEN?

AN INTERACTIVE MONSTER HUNT

BY CRISTINA OXTRA

CAPSTONE PRESS
a capstone imprint

Published by Capstone Press,
an imprint of Capstone.
1710 Roe Crest Drive
North Mankato, Minnesota 56003
capstonepub.com

Library of Congress Cataloging-in-Publication Data is available on the Library of
Congress website
ISBN: 9781666336832 (hardcover)
ISBN: 9781666336849 (paperback)
ISBN: 9781666336856 (ebook PDF)
Library of Congress Control Number: 2022943780

Summary: In this interactive chapter book, YOU are a reporter for a high-profile
magazine, and you're about to discover the greatest scoop yet: Do aliens exist? To
find out, you'll need to investigate some of history's most infamous alien encounters,
from Area 51 in Nevada to Fairbanks, Alaska. Will you discover a real-life alien
being, or will your investigative probe be nothing more than a close encounter?

Editorial Credits
Editor: Donald Lemke; Designer: Sarah Bennett; Media Researcher:
Svetlana Zhurkin; Production Specialist: Katy LaVigne

Image Credits
Alamy: World History Archive, 12; Dreamstime: Roman Krochuk, 74; Getty
Images: Star Tribune/Regene Radniecki, 18, AFP/Bridget Bennett, 63, The
Washington Post/Ash Adams, 77, Beau Rogers, 66, cris180, 69, Zeppelie, 107
(top); NASA, ESA, H. Teplitz and M. Rafelski (IPAC/Caltech), A. Koekemoer
(STScI), R. Windhorst (Arizona State University), and Z. Levay (STScI), 103;
NASA: JPL-Caltech, 101; Shutterstock: adike (alien), cover, 1, Africa Studio, 16,
CanonDLee, 28, Chaikom, 72, Dean Clarke, 58, Dmitry Bezrukov, 14, EQRoy,
93, Fehmiu Roffytavare, 23, Fer Gregory, 84, Fotokita, 82, Ivan Cholakov, 9,
jakkapan, 112 (back), Kalifer–Art Creations, 107 (bottom left), Larry Porges,
52, lassedesignen (creepy street), cover, back cover, 1, Lena_graphics, 106, Marti
Bug Catcher, 89, mkfilm, 36, Nick Fox, 44, Photo Spirit, 98, Rainer Lesniewski,
79, RikoBest, 95, Stock High Angle View, 42, WindVector, 46, Yuriy Mazur, 6;
Wikimedia: Tim Bertelink, 107 (bottom right), U.S. Air Force, 56

TABLE OF CONTENTS

ABOUT YOUR ADVENTURE

You're a small-town reporter who recently landed a job at a big-city magazine. Now you just need a blockbuster assignment to prove you're a top-notch journalist. Then one night, you're watching a TV show about the government's new report on UFOs, or Unidentified Flying Objects. You've always wondered about life beyond Earth—extraterrestrial life. Are aliens real? It'll take all your investigative skills to find out!

Chapter 1 sets the scene. Then you choose which path to read. Follow the directions at the bottom of the page as you read the stories. The decisions you make will change your outcome. After you finish one path, go back and read the others for new perspectives and more adventures!

Turn the page to begin your adventure.

Descriptions of UFOs vary, but many witnesses describe them as large, saucer-like objects in the sky, which explains their nickname, "flying saucers."

ASSIGNMENT: ALIENS

You and fellow reporters are sitting at a U-shaped table waiting for a meeting to begin. Everyone is chatting until the image of your editor, Barbara Chang, pops up on the large video screen at one end of the room. You've admired her since you were a kid watching her on the national news. She reported on major events and interviewed everyone from celebrities to U.S. presidents. You've always wanted to be a reporter, just like Barbara.

Barbara's dark, wavy hair is perfectly styled as always. She is dressed in her usual blouse and blazer. When you were a kid, you'd put on your dad's blazer and stand in front of your bedroom mirror. You'd hold a hairbrush like a microphone and pretend to be Barbara.

Turn the page.

Now she runs her own magazine, and you're working for her.

"Hello, team! Good to see everyone," Barbara says. "This month, we're publishing something new. It's our 'Unexplained Edition,' highlighting mysterious events in the United States. We need story ideas. . . . Anyone?"

One by one, your coworkers call out ideas that include unsolved crimes, medical mysteries, and natural phenomena. Barbara agrees with all of them. Then she looks to you. You're the last one to speak.

"What about our newest reporter?" she asks. "Any ideas?"

Everyone turns to you. You can't believe your luck. This could be the big break you've been waiting for. Mom would be so proud. You take a deep breath before speaking.

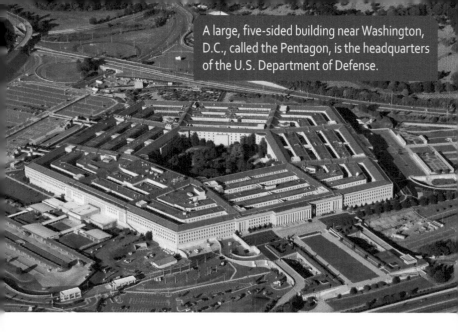

A large, five-sided building near Washington, D.C., called the Pentagon, is the headquarters of the U.S. Department of Defense.

"Well, um, the Department of Defense and the Office of the Director of National Intelligence recently delivered an unclassified report on unidentified flying objects to Congress and—"

Before you can continue, Dudley Fairfax, the magazine's most experienced reporter, laughs. "Really? UFOs? Aliens?" he says. "We're a trustworthy publication—not some trashy rag on a grocery store checkout stand."

Turn the page.

"Actually, the report refers to UFOs as UAPs, or Unidentified Aerial Phenomena," you correct Dudley. "This is a topic the government usually never discusses. Something has changed to warrant declassifying military videos and releasing a report to the public. People want to know more. This could answer the age-old question: Are we alone in the universe?"

"Ha! You're on your own on with this one," Dudley says. "The world doesn't need any more supposed eyewitnesses with unbelievable stories, blurry videos, and photoshopped pictures. It's all hearsay and hoaxes."

"Now, Dudley," Barbara says. "Sounds like this is a hot topic right now. It could get us more readers."

Barbara smiles at you. "The story is yours," she says. "I'm sure you won't disappoint."

You swallow hard, force a smile, and shake your head. You hope you haven't bitten off more than you can chew. You can't let your idol down. Dudley smirks.

Barbara turns to the rest of the reporters. "Thanks, everyone. Now get going. You have deadlines to meet!"

Everyone scrambles to their feet and scurries in different directions. At your desk, you read the government report online. It's based on a task force's review of 144 UAP reports made by military aviators between 2004 and 2021. Of those reports, the task force could only determine an explanation for one—a deflated balloon. The rest remains unexplained.

You watch the videos showing military pilots encountering UAPs and describing what they are seeing. Could these be aliens flying in our airspace?

Turn the page.

Disk Craze Continues

Army Disk-ounts New Mexico Find As Weather Gear

FORT WORTH, July 9.—(JP)—An examination by the Army revealed last night that a mysterious object found on a lonely New Mexico ranch was a harmless high-altitude weather balloon—not a grounded flying disk.

Excitement was high in disk-conscious Texas until Brig Gen. Roger M. Ramey, commander of the Eight Air Forces with headquarters here cleared up the mystery.

The bundle of tinfoil, broken wood beams and rubber remnants of a ballon was sent here yesterday by army air transport in the wake of reports that it was a flying disk.

But the general said the objects were the crushed remains of a Ray wind target used to determine the direction and velocity of winds at high altitudes.

Warrant Officer Irving Newton, forecaster at the Army Air Forces weather station here, said "we use them because they go much higher than the eye can see."

NOT A FLYING DISC—Major. Jesse A. Marcel of Houma, La., intelligence officer of the 509th Bomb Group at Roswell, New Mexico, inspects what was identified by a Fort Worth, Texas, Army Air Base weather forecaster as a ray wind target used to determine the direction and velocity of winds at high altitudes. Initial stories originating from Roswell, where the object was found, had labelled it a "flying disc" but inspection at Fort Worth revealed its true nature. (AP Wirephoto).

A newspaper article dismissed the supposed crash of a UFO in Roswell, New Mexico, in 1947.

Perhaps the most famous alleged UFO sighting occurred on July 7, 1947. A rancher reported finding what he thought was the crash site of a flying saucer near Roswell, New Mexico. When he told officials at the Roswell Army Airfield, they issued a press release claiming they had retrieved a flying saucer.

The next day, the Air Force took back the claim, explaining it was a misidentified weather balloon. Some believe that was a coverup, and the downed spacecraft along with the aliens onboard were whisked away and hidden at a highly secured military installation in Nevada called Area 51.

For many years, there have also been claims of alien sightings across the country. The state with the most reports of UFO sightings in the past 50 years is Alaska. There have been more than 6,500 reports. Many come from the city of Fairbanks in the central part of the state. Could aliens be frequent visitors in Alaska?

You look into your home state, Minnesota, and discover there have been sightings there too. On August 27, 1979, in Warren, Minnesota, Sheriff's Deputy Val Johnson was on patrol early in the morning when he saw a bright light.

Turn the page.

Light pillars are a natural phenomenon that occur when light reflects off floating ice crystals, but people often mistake them for alien life.

As he approached it, the light beamed through the windshield hitting him and knocking him out. He called police dispatch and reported that something attacked his car. He said glass broke and the brakes locked.

According to the sheriff's office reports, Johnson's wristwatch and the clock in his cruiser stopped for 14 minutes. He said his teeth were fractured at the gumline and his eyes burned. As proof of this event, his damaged squad car is on display at the Marshall County Historical Society Museum.

After more than an hour of researching, you head to the watercooler to fill up your water bottle. When you return, you find a Post-it note stuck to your computer screen. The message reads, "This is not going to be easy, and it could be dangerous. Beware of those who may sabotage you. Good luck!"

Turn the page.

This is not going to be easy, and it could be dangerous. Beware of those who may sabotage you. Good luck!

You don't recognize the handwriting, and everyone uses the same office-issued Post-it notes. You peek over your cubicle and look around the office. Everyone is busy. It's probably Dudley pulling a prank.

"I'll show him," you mumble. You sit back down and consider three places to explore for your story.

You know that this decision cannot be taken lightly.

To visit the Twin Cities, Minnesota, turn to page 19.
To travel to Area 51, Nevada, turn to page 45.
To venture to Fairbanks, Alaska, turn to page 75.

In 1979, Marshall County Sheriff's Deputy Val Johnson reported seeing a UFO in the sky above Oslo, Minnesota.

CHAPTER 2

NORTHERN EXPOSURE

"When you moved to write for that magazine, I thought you'd be writing about big news, interviewing famous people, or maybe meeting the president," your mom says. She sits across from you at the breakfast table. You're staying with her while you're in Minnesota. "But UFOs? Aliens? That's not what I expected."

"You sound like my coworker Dudley," you say while splashing your scrambled eggs with hot sauce and then slathering lingonberry jam on toast. "I plan to meet someone later to talk about UFO and alien sightings in Minnesota. When I uncover the truth about extraterrestrials, it *will* be big news! It'll be the biggest news in the world!"

Turn the page.

Mom cups her hands around her coffee mug and frowns. "You remind me of your Uncle Jack," she says. "He said he saw aliens in the cornfield."

You stop in mid-chew. "You didn't tell me that! When did that happen?" you ask.

"He was a teenager then. After saying he saw aliens, he refused to go in the fields. That made your Grandpa Gus mad because he thought he was just trying to get out of working," Mom explains. "Eventually, word got out in town, and everyone heard about it. People avoided him. Kids called him names, like Spaceman Jack. When he met your Aunt Rosita, she asked him to stop talking about it, and he did. He has kept that promise ever since."

"Do you think he'd talk to me about it?" you ask.

"Maybe. Your aunt is out of town this week," Mom says. "Just don't cause him any trouble, all right?"

"Of course not," you say. "I've got two possible leads. Uncle Jack and the president of a group that investigates reports of UFOs and aliens." You smile at Mom. "See, Mom," you say. "I *am* meeting famous people and presidents."

To visit Uncle Jack, turn to page 22.

To meet the president of a UFO and alien encounters group, turn to page 38.

Late that afternoon, you drive for an hour in your rental car to visit Uncle Jack. He still lives in the small town he grew up in. You tell him about your story for the magazine.

"Your Aunt Rosita would not be happy to hear me talking about this," he says.

"I know. Mom told me," you say. "I really need this story, Uncle Jack. Maybe you can be an anonymous source." You take out your pen and notebook. "Please, can you tell me what happened that night?"

"I got into an argument with my dad, your Grandpa Gus, one evening. I ran out of the house and into the cornfields across the road. I just wanted to get away," Uncle Jack recalls. "But I got lost in the maze of tall cornstalks. Then I saw a bright light beaming above the stalks. I walked toward it thinking it was the way out. Then . . . I saw them."

"Them?" you echo.

"The aliens," he says. "I didn't see their faces. Just two silhouettes. They were short and had large heads, skinny legs, and thin arms."

"What did you do?" you ask.

Turn the page.

"I froze for a moment and then realized I'd better get out of there," Uncle Jack says. "I turned around and started running. But I still couldn't figure my way out, so I hid among the cornstalks, shaking and praying they wouldn't see me. My dad and my brothers later found me curled up tight, shivering in the dirt among the stalks."

"That must've been terrifying!" you say. "Does our family still own the farm?"

"No. When Dad got sick a few years later and no one in the family wanted to take it over, he sold it to some businessmen who wanted to build a bed and breakfast," Uncle Jack explains. "They tore down the grain silo and brought in a crew of workers, but that's as far as they got. The bed and breakfast was never built. For some reason, the work stopped. They still own the land today and haven't sold it to anyone else."

"Can you take me there?" you ask.

Uncle Jack sighs and scratches his bald head. "I avoid even driving past the place," he says. "But I know this is important to you. . . . You'll have to drive. I don't see well at night anymore." He points to his thick-rimmed glasses.

One the way to the farm, you stop at a gas station. Uncle Jack offers to buy slushies, like he used to when you were a kid visiting him and Aunt Rosita. Two men enter the store after you. They're dressed in jeans, boots, camouflage jackets, and baseball caps. Not an unusual site in the area.

At the slushie machine, you fill up tall plastic cups for you and Uncle Jack. One of the men grabs an empty cup.

"I've never had one of these before," he says to you. "Which flavor is the best?"

Turn the page.

"Never?" you say. "I like mixing blue cola with cherry."

Uncle Jack leans in. "Do I know you?" he asks the man.

"Don't think so. We're just passing through," says the man. "Got back from hunting and heading home. Didn't get anything."

"Maybe next time," Uncle Jack says.

He turns to you. "Come on, let's go," he says as he ushers you to the cashier. He quickly pays for the slushies and you both leave.

"Are we in a rush?" you ask as you get into the car and drive away.

"Those men give me the heebie-jeebies," Uncle Jack says. "They remind me of two creepy men I met a few days after I saw the aliens."

Uncle Jack explains, "I was at the hardware store on an errand for my dad when these men in dark suits approached me. They said they heard about my experience and kept asking me about it. They were intense—like they were questioning me about a crime."

"Did they threaten you?" you ask.

"They told me I should stop talking because people would think I'm crazy, and it would only make my life and others around me miserable," Uncle Jack says. "It was such a horrible thing to say. I bought what I needed and got out of there fast. I never saw them again after that."

"Thank goodness!" you say.

You reach the farm a few minutes later. You park on the dirt path in front of an old farmhouse with boarded-up windows and peeling, once-white paint.

Turn the page.

Ivy vines have snaked their way up and wrapped around the home. The roof on the weather-beaten and timeworn barn has long since collapsed and several pieces of its wooden walls are missing.

"It's sad to see the old home like this," Uncle Jack says.

You pat him on the shoulder.

The two of you stroll around the farm. You take pictures with your digital camera while Uncle Jack tells stories of growing up on the farm. As the sun sets, you notice strange flashing balls of light in the sky across the road. "Look, Uncle Jack, what's that?" you ask.

The lights hover above an overgrown field. You take pictures of them.

"I don't like this," Uncle Jack says, nudging you toward the car. "Let's go."

You snap one more picture before getting into the car where your uncle is already buckled in and ready to leave. You strap on your safety belt, insert the key in the ignition, and are about to start the car. Suddenly, a blinding light surrounds you, Uncle Jack, and the car.

"Argh!" you cry out, shutting your eyes and shielding them with your arms.

Turn the page.

The car starts rocking violently as though giant hands were shaking it to empty its contents. The cups of slushies spill all over the car. The headlights flash on and off, and the windshield wipers swoosh back and forth across the windshield.

"I know you want this story, but I can't do this!" Uncle Jack shouts. "Let's get out of here! Drive! Now!"

To drive away, turn to page 31.

To stay, turn to page 33.

A large crack appears at a corner of the car's windshield. You're afraid it will spread and shatter entirely. Uncle Jack is sweating and quivering. He yells, "Let's go! Drive away now!"

You slam on the accelerator. The wheels spin as they struggle to get traction on the dirt before the car finally speeds off.

A few minutes later, the headlights stop flashing, and the windshield wipers stop swiping. Your heart is pounding as though you had just run a marathon. Uncle Jack is sweating, breathing hard, and has both hands over his heart. Neither you nor he speak until you reach the driveway at his house.

There, you scroll through the photos in your camera. "No!" you exclaim. "All the photos are overexposed!" You can't see anything on them. You lower your head and grumble, "I can just hear Dudley laughing at me right now."

Turn the page.

"Who?" Uncle Jack asks.

"Someone who'd be happy I failed," you reply. "This reminds me of that UFO case I read about in Warren." You tell him the story. You blink your eyes and check your gums. "At least the light didn't burn my eyes or injure my gums, like the deputy sheriff in Warren."

"We shouldn't have come here. If your Aunt Rosita finds out, she's not going to like this," Uncle Jack says.

You stare at the cracked windshield on the rental car and the blue and red slushie stains all over the interior. The magazine will have to pay for damages to the car. "Barbara isn't going to like this either," you say.

THE END

To read another, turn to page 17.
To learn more about aliens, turn to page 106.

"One more picture," you say as you raise your camera up.

No sooner have you uttered those words when you feel a sharp pain at the back of your neck. Was the light doing this to them?

"Ow!" you howl.

Uncle Jack's voice lowers. "I . . . I . . . can't move . . . and I'm . . . having a hard time . . . breathing. Call . . . 911." He closes his eyes.

"Uncle Jack!" You shake him, but he doesn't respond. You feel dizzy as you fish your phone from your pocket. But your fingers go numb, and you drop the phone. You fumble for it as your eyes begin to feel so heavy that you're forced to close them.

You open your eyes. The car is still. The headlights aren't flashing. The windshield wipers aren't moving. There is no bright light.

Turn the page.

All is still and silent. Your head is spinning, and your body aches. You look to Uncle Jack whose eyes are still shut and shake him. "Uncle Jack! Wake up! Are you all right?"

His eyes pop open, and he gasps. "Huh? What . . . What happened?"

"Oh, thank goodness! You're OK!" you say, hugging him.

"Um . . . not quite," he says. He turns away, flings the car door open, and throws up on the ground. "My stomach is churning like a washing machine, and every bone in my body hurts. How long was I passed out for?"

You look at your watch in disbelief. "It's been three hours since we saw the light," you say. "We both passed out. I don't remember anything after that."

"I don't either," Uncle Jack says as he shuts the car door. He wipes his lips with the sleeve of his plaid shirt.

"Wait. I drove here," you say.

"Of course, you did. I don't drive at night," Uncle Jack says. He takes off his eyeglasses and examines the crack on one of the lenses. "How did I break that?"

"So why am I in the passenger seat, and you're in the driver seat?" you ask. Neither of you recall switching places.

You pick up your camera that had fallen at your feet and wipe off the spilled slushie with your hands. Then you scroll through the pictures you took earlier, hoping to find clues as to what happened. But every picture is too bright, overexposed. You can't see anything in them.

Turn the page.

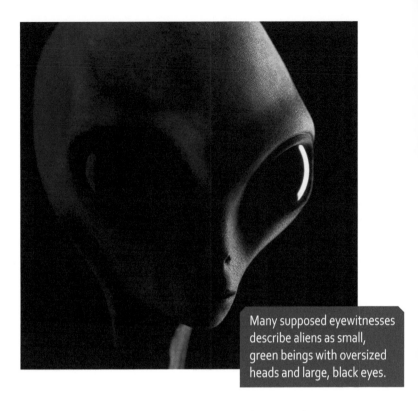

Many supposed eyewitnesses describe aliens as small, green beings with oversized heads and large, black eyes.

Except for the last picture. It shows what appears to be two pairs of deep-set, large black eyes staring into the camera. No other facial features show. Everything else around them is dark. They don't look like human eyes.

"Uncle Jack, look!" you say passing the camera to him.

He stares at the picture. "It's . . . it's them, isn't it?" he mumbles. His hands tremble as he returns the camera to you.

"I've heard of stories like this—bright lights, unexplained time lapse, and memory loss. They're usually related to alien abductions," you say. "Were we abducted by aliens and then accidentally returned in the wrong seats?"

Uncle Jack shudders. "Your Aunt Rosita is not going to believe this," he says.

You point at the picture in the camera. "Will anyone believe us?" you add.

THE END

To read another, turn to page 17.
To learn more about aliens, turn to page 106.

Later in the evening, you head to a public library to attend a meeting of a group called S.T.A.R.S., the Search for Truth and Alien Research Society, which investigates UFO and alien sightings. You're welcomed by the group's president, Zoe Smith, whom you interviewed on the phone earlier.

"Have a seat anywhere you'd like. I told everyone you're coming," Zoe says. "Our meeting is members only. We've gotten some weird people in the past when we opened it up to anyone. If you have any questions, please let us know. We'd be happy to help."

You take a seat in the back row. Zoe adjusts her cat-eye frame glasses and primps her curly dark hair. Then she heads to the front of the room. She stands beside a projector screen and presents the number of reported UFO and alien sightings for the month.

Various group members have investigated and debunked almost all the reports—except for two that have yet to be investigated. After the meeting, you decide to investigate one of these cases. The location of alleged repeated UFO sightings was only a few minutes' drive away, so you head there.

Turn the page.

When you arrive at the location, you realize it's near an airport where small aircraft and helicopters take off and land regularly. You sit in your car listening to the radio while observing the sky for anything out of the ordinary.

An hour later, nothing has happened.

To go to Area 51, Nevada, turn to page 45.

To go to Fairbanks, Alaska, turn to page 75.

To wait a little longer, turn to page 41.

You wait another half hour when you see strange blinking lights. First there's only one set of lights. But then another set appears. They dip and dive in a way that aircraft don't. You get out of the car and start taking pictures with your camera.

"Jackpot! Wait until Dudley sees this!" you exclaim.

When you walk over to the next block to get closer shots, you observe two young men standing in the front yard of a home. They're gazing up at the sky and watching the lights.

"Great! Eyewitnesses!" you say.

You approach them. "Excuse me. What are those lights up there?"

The men turn around, and you notice they are each holding remote control.

Turn the page.

Some people fly drones, also known as unmanned aerial vehicles, as a hobby.

One of them replies, "Oh, you like our drones? Pretty cool, huh?"

"We fly them late at night, so we don't get in trouble with the airport," the other man says. "Are you taking pictures of them?"

"Drones? No. I thought. . . . Never mind," you say with your head hanging low. "Sorry to bother you."

You head back to your car. "That was embarrassing," you think aloud. "I'd better investigate somewhere else."

THE END

To read another, turn to page 17.
To learn more about aliens, turn to page 106.

Rachel, Nevada, the closest town to Area 51, is known as the UFO Capital of the World.

CHAPTER 3
SECURED SECRETS

The sun is setting when you meet Stewart Gordon at the Little A'Le'Inn, in Rachel, Nevada. You had read an interesting article that Stewart wrote for a website for alien enthusiasts. He is a Nevada historian and university professor who thinks Area 51 could be holding extraterrestrial secrets.

Located 147 miles from Las Vegas, the inn is made up of a motel, souvenir shop, and restaurant. It's the last stop to get food, water, and souvenirs before reaching Area 51. The sign outside the inn reads, "Earthlings Welcome." Next to it is a pickup truck with a crane holding up a model of an alien spacecraft. A mural shows spacecraft, aliens, and an image of Area 51.

Turn the page.

The sign at the door boasts the inn's restaurant menu which includes "the famous alien burger."

The restaurant is decorated with artwork featuring more aliens and alien spacecraft. You and Stewart sit at a table and order drinks. You notice two men sitting a few feet away eating burgers and fries.

Area 51 is a military base located in a remote part of southern Nevada.

The men appear to resemble the people you had seen earlier at your hotel. They were in the hotel lobby, at the breakfast buffet, and in the gift shop. The men you saw at the hotel wore black suits. These men in the restaurant are wearing jeans, hoodies, and baseball caps pulled over their eyes.

To talk to the two men, turn to page 48.

To ignore the men and focus on listening to Stewart, turn to page 55.

"Excuse me," you tell Stewart. "I have to talk to someone."

You approach the men. "Hi. Do I know you?" you ask. "Are you following me?"

They stare at you blankly. "No," one of the men replies. He turns to his companion. "Do you know this person?"

The other man shakes his head.

You continue questioning them. "Did Dudley put you up to this?"

"Who?" they ask in unison.

One of the men says, "Maybe we should ask who you are and why you're bothering us."

"I'm a reporter doing a story on Area 51," you reply. "I'm wondering why I keep seeing you everywhere I go since I arrived in Vegas."

The men laugh.

"You're not the only one who comes here looking for aliens," one of them says. "My brother and I are on vacation. We're here to have fun and tell family and friends back home we've been to Area 51."

The second man adds, "We're also here for dinner, and you're ruining it."

A waitress approaches. "Is everything all right, gentlemen?" she asks the men. "Are you with them?" she asks you.

"We've never seen this person before," one of the men says.

"Can you please return to your table?" the waitress asks you.

You look across the room and see a customer whip out a cell phone and point it in your direction. You don't want a video of you posted on social media.

Turn the page.

"I'm sorry. I must be mistaken," you tell the men and then quickly return to your table.

"What's going on?" Stewart asks.

"I swear I've seen them at the hotel where I'm staying," you whisper. "I think they're following me."

The two men stand up. One of them places cash on their table and tells the waitress, "Ma'am, we're sorry. We've lost our appetites."

The waitress apologizes and offers to pack their food for them to go.

"It's OK. It's not your fault," he says and hands her money. "Here. For your troubles."

The waitress looks at the cash. "This is quite a tip! Thank you."

From a window by your table, you watch as the men get into a silver four-door sedan.

You turn away briefly to sip your iced tea and then look again. As their car reverses out of its parking space, you can't believe what you see in the car. Two gray faces with barely visible noses, tiny mouths, and large dark eyes.

You spring from your seat and shout, "Look, Stewart! Look!" You point at the car.

You don't notice that you've knocked over his glass of soda, which spills onto his lap. "Argh!" he yowls.

"Stewart, look!" you yell again.

But he's too busy wiping the soda from his lap with a soggy napkin.

The car speeds away when Stewart looks out the window. "What are you looking at?" he asks. "I don't see anything."

"Aliens!" you burst out.

Turn the page.

A group of alien models at the International UFO Museum and Research Center in Roswell, New Mexico

Diners sitting on stools spin around to see what is happening. Customers and staff freeze. The clinking of utensils stops. No one moves or talks. Everything grinds to a halt.

The waitress approaches you again. "You're disrupting our customers, and I'll have to ask you to leave," she says.

You turn to Stewart. "I saw them! Those men are aliens!" you insist.

Stewart's face reddens. "Listen. I don't know what you're getting at. I agreed to help you and take you to see Area 51 to examine facts and investigate scientifically. I don't work with people like this," he says. "Sorry. You'll have to find someone else to help you. I'm out."

"Wait! I'm sorry! Come back!" you call out.

Stewart is not convinced. "You're on your own," he says and walks away.

Turn the page.

His words sting and remind you of Dudley who had told you the same thing. You question yourself. Were the men aliens? Was it a trick of the mind? Or the fading light outside? Was it real or a joke?

You don't think you can go to Area 51 without Stewart. Now what?

THE END

To read another, turn to page 17.
To learn more about aliens, turn to page 106.

You figure it's just a coincidence. You take notes while Stewart provides background information about Area 51.

"The entire complex that includes Area 51 with its hangars, dormitories, radar tower, runways, munitions area, and explosion proof building, is the size of Rhode Island and Connecticut combined," he explains. "Before it was called Area 51, the government took over the area known as Groom Lake for military use during World War II. In 1955, the Central Intelligence Agency chose Groom Lake as a site for testing the classified U-2 spy plane, so a runway ideal for the plane was built. More facilities, runways, and buildings were later added to test other aircraft."

According to Stewart, by the 1960s, the base became the center for the development and testing of top-secret military aircraft.

Turn the page.

The A-12, also known as the A-12 Oxcart, was a U.S. military spy plane.

The A-12, F-117, and B-2 Bomber were all developed at the base. It also tested captured Soviet aircraft. In the 1980s, alleged government physicist Bob Lazar claimed he worked on the base and that part of Area 51 houses aliens and alien spacecraft. But there are no photos or videos to support his claims.

"The CIA finally acknowledged Area 51's existence in 2013," Stewart says. "Although the airspace around it is still strictly controlled."

"High security," you say.

"Extremely," Stewart answers.

According to Stewart, stories abound about elite security forces referred to as "Camo Dudes" because they usually wear camouflage gear.

"Helicopters and jets patrol the area. There are also sensors that collect audio and visual data across that area of the desert," Stewart adds. "Don't worry. I've been there before. We'll be all right. Let's go. We'll take my jeep. The terrain is rough out there."

You and Stewart head to Highway 375, nicknamed the Extraterrestrial Highway, to reach Groom Lake Road. This dirt road leads directly to Area 51.

Turn the page.

When you reach the northeast area of Area
51, you observe mountains in the distance.
Closer to you are tall metal fences surrounded
by signs warning people to keep away, like
"U.S. Air Force Installation. Restricted Area,"
"No Trespassing Beyond This Point," and
"Photography Is Prohibited."

Yet you grab your camera and prepare to take pictures. As you scan the desert surroundings composed of sand, dirt, rocks, and dehydrated vegetation, you spot two headlights. It's a dark pickup truck perched at the top of a hill.

"Someone's up there," you point out to Stewart.

"Camo Dudes," he says. "Are you all right to stay? It's OK if you don't. Maybe we can go somewhere else to get another view."

To stay, turn to page 60.

If Stewart suggests an alternative and you agree, turn to page 65.

"Yeah, I can stay. I need this story," you say.

You start snapping photos as you slowly creep forward. You train your camera on the pickup truck on the hill. You are about to take a picture when you're startled by a siren. A police car with red, white, and blue lights flashing and siren blaring speeds toward you and Stewart.

"Great," Stewart mutters. "I've never had cops stop me here before."

An officer gets out of the police car and approaches you and Stewart. You hide the camera behind your back.

"Good evening, Officer," Stewart says.

The officer does not acknowledge Stewart's greeting. "This is a military installation," he says. "You can't hang around here."

You look up at the pickup truck on the hill. You see figures inside the vehicle.

"Did they call you?" you ask. "I'm a reporter doing a story about Area 51. I can show you my media credentials. My friend here is helping me."

"It doesn't matter who either of you are," the officer says. "You can't be here, and you can't take pictures. Let me see that camera behind your back."

You sigh and offer the camera to the officer. He scrolls through the photos then points to one of the posted signs. "See? It says no photography."

"Fine. We won't take any pictures," you say.

The officer hands the camera back to you. "Get out here, the both of you, before I arrest you for trespassing," he says.

Turn the page.

Stewart hooks his arms around yours. "Yes, sir. We were just leaving," he says.

"But . . . but . . ." you sputter.

"Let's go," Stewart whispers. "I have a job and reputation to keep. I'm sure you want to do the same."

The officer watches as you and Stewart drive away. "I'm sorry it didn't work out," he says. "Maybe another night."

"I only have one night here," you say.

Stewart shrugs. "I guess better luck next time."

He drops you off at the A'Le'Inn where your car is parked, and you return to your hotel. In your room, you check the photos in your camera. But there are no photos.

"No! No! No!" you exclaim.

Visitors gather outside the Little A'Le'Inn in Rachel, Nevada.

You discover the memory card on which the photos are stored is missing. Maybe it fell out when the police officer grabbed the camera or when you took it back from him.

Or could he have taken it?

Turn the page.

Your phone buzzes.

Barbara texted you, saying, "Checking in. Hope your story is going well."

You collapse onto your bed and groan. "This is a dead end."

THE END

To read another, turn to page 17.
To learn more about aliens, turn to page 106.

"We can go somewhere else where no one is likely to bother us. You'll get a faraway view of Area 51, but it might be better than getting run off by Camo Dudes," he suggests. "We can hike to the summit of Tikaboo Peak."

"Hike at night?" you ask.

"It's a mile hike and a 1,000-foot ascent over some steep terrain, but it's the only location to legally view the base," Stewart says. "I went on a hike with a friend last weekend, and I've got gear for two still in the jeep. The best time to see Area 51 from the summit is at sunrise."

"I don't have that much time. I'm on deadline, and I leave early tomorrow morning. Tonight is all I have," you say. "Glad I wore my best boots and have my extra zoom lens in my backpack. Let's go!"

Turn the page.

After a 26-mile drive, you and Stewart reach Tikaboo Peak and begin the hike to the top. It is a slow and scary ascent, especially in the dark. Fortunately, Stewart has helmets equipped with headlamps to guide the way. At some points, you crawl on your hands and knees through loose rocks and dirt.

View of Area 51 from Tikaboo Peak in Lincoln County, Nevada

When you finally reach the top of Tikaboo Peak, you train your camera lens toward Area 51. You zoom in as much as you can and faintly see hints of a runway, buildings, and lights.

Click! Click! You snap pictures.

"Hold on. What are those?" Stewart asks, pointing to the night sky.

Strange cylinder-shaped lights appear. At first, they just float—not moving. Then they start zipping by at incredible speed without a sound. No aircraft engine. Not a single noise. Just a quiet but impressive light show.

You snap more pictures. *Click! Click!*

"Could they be . . . UFOs?" you ask.

Stewart is speechless as he stares at the sky entranced by the lights.

Turn the page.

A much larger triangular arrangement of red and gold lights emerges seemingly from out of nowhere and hovers above the other lights. The smaller lights swirl around it. Then, as quickly as all the lights appeared, they vanish.

"Where did they go?" Stewart asks, spinning around and searching the sky.

"I think they're gone," you tell Stewart and then laugh. "No planes can move like that! They had to be alien spacecraft, and I got them on camera! Can't wait for Dudley to see these!"

"Who?" Stewart asks.

"Someone who doesn't believe I can pull this off," you answer.

"Well, you did! Good job!" Stewart says. You high-five one another. "Come on. We have a long hike down."

Turn the page.

You are nearing the bottom of the peak when you slip and tumble down, stopping among a clump of rocks.

Stewart runs to your aid. "Are you OK?"

You try to get up and feel a sharp pain in your left foot. "Ow," you say, grimacing and cringing. You collapse back on the ground.

Stewart helps you hobble back to the jeep and calls 911 on his cell phone. A few minutes later, an ambulance arrives. Two medics help you onto a gurney.

You look closely at them. "Do I know you?" you ask them.

"I think you may have a head injury," one of the medics says. "Don't worry. You'll be all right. We'll take you to the hospital."

The medics load you into the ambulance.

"I'll meet you at the hospital," Stewart says.

As the ambulance drives off with you inside, one of the medics takes your arm and gives you a shot. You hear him say, "This will help take the edge off." Then you drift off to sleep.

Later, you wake up in a bed in a hospital room. Every muscle in your body is sore, and you have a headache. Stewart is beside you.

Turn the page.

"Hey," he says. "The doctor says you're lucky. A sprained ankle, a broken toe, and a few cuts and bruises. No concussion or serious injuries."

You look at your bandaged ankle and toe. "At least we still have the pictures," you say.

"About that . . ." Stewart starts. He opens your backpack and takes out your shattered camera. "It was damaged when you fell. It won't turn on, and the memory card is gone."

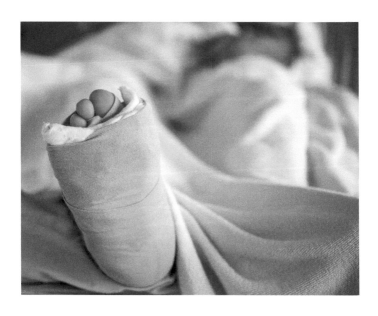

"Nooooo! It can be!" you exclaim. You cover your face with your hands and picture in your mind Barbara and your mom shaking their heads at you in disappointment. "I'm doomed."

THE END

To read another, turn to page 17.
To learn more about aliens, turn to page 106.

Aurora borealis, also called northern lights, is a natural light display seen in the sky above northern regions of Earth.

CHAPTER 4

CABIN IN THE WOODS

Through your research, you read about
Clara Wright, a divorced bank manager living
in Fairbanks who claims to have had an alien
encounter. You arrange to meet her.

At the airport, as you stand in line preparing
to board your flight, you notice two men wearing
black suits and dark sunglasses. They are sitting
in the waiting area nearby. One is reading a
book, and the other is reading a newspaper. You
wonder how they could read with those glasses.
You shake your head and board your plane.

At a hotel in Fairbanks, you put on a sweater
and coat. Then you meet Clara, a brown-haired,
soft-spoken woman in her mid-thirties. You hop
in her red pickup truck and head for her house.

Turn the page.

On the way, you ask her questions and take notes. "I've read Alaska is the top state in reports of UFO encounters. Why do you think that is?" you say.

"There are several theories," Clara replies. "Alaska is a large state, but it also has the least amount of people. There is barely 15,000 miles of roads in the entire state and more than 365,000 miles of waterways. You've got to have a boat or a plane to get to many of the isolated places here. It's a good place to hide or do something you don't want anyone to see."

"You think aliens are watching people here?" you ask.

"Possibly," Clara replies. "There are nine military bases in Alaska. Elmendorf Air Force Base, Fort Richardson, and Fort Wainwright in Fairbanks are the largest. Maybe aliens are interested in our military."

Turn the page.

Clara continues, "They want to see what technology we have. Maybe they want to know whether we pose a threat to them or the rest of the universe."

"Is it possible that what people are reporting are aircraft?" you ask. "Maybe experimental aircraft or weapons the military doesn't want anyone to know about?"

"That's also possible," Clara says. "But many of the descriptions of UFOs don't match any known military aircraft. There are also reports of alien abductions."

"How often do you think alien abductions happen in Alaska?" you ask.

"There have been many reports. That's from those who came back," Clara says. "I'm sure you've heard of the Bermuda Triangle, where ships and airplanes disappear."

"Of course," you reply.

"We have the Alaska Triangle," Clara says. "It's a stretch of untouched wilderness that connects the state's largest city of Anchorage to Juneau in the southeast and then to Barrow, a town on the state's north coast."

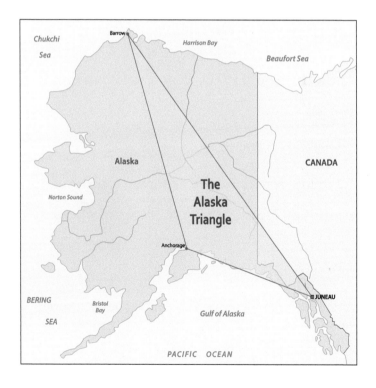

Turn the page.

"Since 1988, more than 16,000 people have vanished in that area," Clara continues. "It has a missing-person rate at more than twice the national average. Some believe these missing people have been taken by aliens."

You think about Dudley. What alien would want him? They'd probably listen to him prattle on for a few minutes then kick him out of their spacecraft!

"Why would aliens want to take humans?" you ask.

"Some say it's for scientific purposes. To study us," Clara says. "Humans study plants and creatures on Earth to gain a better understanding of our world, to learn more about life, how to prevent or cure illnesses, and how to protect the environment. Maybe they're doing the same?"

Clara turns on to a tree-lined gravel road and follows it uphill toward her home. "Here we are. Welcome to my little hideaway home."

"It's lovely!" you say.

You marvel at the gingerbread-colored log cabin with a ridged, chocolate-brown roof topped by a chimney. The windows are trimmed in forest green, which matches the front door that's decorated with a wreath of fall leaves. A wooden rocking chair, a table with a lantern, a colorful doormat, and potted plants decorate the front porch.

"I was sitting right there." Clara points at the porch. "Relaxing with my dog Roscoe when I saw what looked like a big, bright star shoot down into the woods across from the house."

Clara said she didn't think anything was wrong until she heard rustling in the woods.

Turn the page.

"I heard leaves crunching, like someone was walking toward the house. Roscoe started growling and barking. We went back in the house and locked the door," she recalls. "I observed from the living room window to see if anyone or anything would appear. That's when I saw several figures. Silhouettes. I couldn't see faces or clothing. I'm five-foot-six, and they were shorter than me. Less than five feet. They had large heads with slender arms and legs."

"Did you take any pictures? Call for help?" you ask.

"No. I don't have a home phone. I forgot to charge my cell phone and it was dead, so I couldn't call anyone or take pictures," Clara says. "As they closed in on my house, my motion sensor lights outside turned on. It aimed a beam of light at them. I thought I'd see who or what they were. But in a blink of an eye, they were gone. I went from window to window in the house searching, but there was no sign of anyone. I stayed in my room huddled in bed with Roscoe beside me."

"How frightening!" you say.

"It gets stranger. I saw a light shine through the bedroom window and heard humming in my ears. Roscoe yelped and ran out of the room. Then nothing," she says.

Turn the page.

Clara adds, "I don't remember anything after that. I thought I might've fallen asleep. I woke up two hours later with a headache and a nosebleed. Roscoe was beside me whimpering. I had a hard time sleeping that night. The next morning, I went into the woods looking to see if there was anything that would clue me in on what happened. But there was nothing."

"Can we go in the woods, so I can take pictures?" you ask. Clara agrees.

As you are about to head into the woods, Clara's phone rings. It's her cousin, and they talk. When Clara hangs up, she tells you she needs to help her cousin urgently. "She only lives half an hour away. I'm sorry. I won't be long."

Clara leads you into her house, and you're greeted by Roscoe, Clara's friendly golden retriever. He runs up to you and wags his tail.

"Make yourself comfortable. I prepared some cheese, crackers, fruit, and drinks for your visit. They're on the dining table. Help yourself," Clara says. "Roscoe will keep you company."

Roscoe barks twice, seeming to understand and accept his assignment.

Clara leaves.

Turn the page.

An hour passes. You've eaten, looked around Clara's house, checked your email on your phone, and taken pictures of Roscoe. And Clara has not returned yet. You peek out of the living room window. It's now ink-black outside.

You are about to turn away when you notice bright lights rocketing down from the sky and into the woods across from the house.

If you stay put and call for help, turn to page 87.
If you head into the woods, turn to page 89.

You worry the lights may be from an aircraft crashing in the woods and someone may be hurt. You are about to call 911 when you see a police car driving toward the house. You hurry outside to identify yourself and tell them what you saw.

"We got a call about the same thing. That's why we're here," one of the officers says. "We'll check it out."

One officer heads off into the woods while the other stays with you. As you look at him closely, he reminds you of someone, but you can't remember who. "You look familiar. I think you both do," you say. "Maybe I met you recently? Somewhere outside of Alaska?"

"I doubt that. My partner and I haven't had time off in weeks, let alone travel out of state," he says. "It's probably one of the military planes just flying by. We have many of them around here. Even us locals can make a mistake."

Turn the page.

When the other officer returns, he says he didn't see anything unusual in the woods. "No offense, but this place can be a lot to take in all at once for city folks," he says.

"No offense taken," you say. "Just wanted to be sure it wasn't anything serious. Thanks for checking it out."

After they leave, you go inside, lock the door, and call Clara. When she returns, you grab flashlights and venture into the woods hoping to find some clues as to what you may have seen. But neither of you find anything. You leave Fairbanks the next day disappointed.

THE END

To read another, turn to page 17.
To learn more about aliens, turn to page 106.

You grab your camera and rush out the door. Roscoe follows, but you instruct him to stay in the house then close the door. The motion sensor light outside turns on as you cross its path and enter the woods.

Deeper among the trees, the motion sensor light is no longer able to help you see your way, so you turn on the flashlight on your phone. You see a pulsating white light ahead and go toward it. Before you can reach it, you see two figures standing among the trees, silhouetted by the light behind them.

Turn the page.

y are human-like but have larger
nd long arms and legs. Like in Clara's
descriptions.

You hide behind a rock and aim your camera toward the figures. But then you start feeling a headache spreading from the back of your head to the front. You try to ignore it and stay focused on taking pictures.

To go back to the house, turn to page 91.
To stay in the woods, turn to page 94.

The headache gets sharper. You call Clara and whisper into the phone. "Something . . . woods," you say. "Like . . . you said . . . I'm . . ."

"What? I can't hear you. You sound garbled. What about the woods?" Clara says, "You don't sound well. Stay in the house. I'll call for help."

Dizzily, you stagger out to the entrance to the woods before collapsing to the ground.

Later, you're awakened by Clara shaking you and two police officers standing beside her.

"Thank goodness you're OK!" Clara says. "You scared me, so I called the cops."

You look at the two police officers. "Thanks for coming." You pause, then ask, "Do I know you? Have I seen you somewhere before recently?"

One of the officers chuckles.

Turn the page.

"My partner and I haven't had time off in weeks, let alone travel out of state," he says. "Here, let me help you up. Are you OK?"

You tell them what you saw in the woods. "I'll show you," you say. You scroll through the pictures in your camera, but there isn't a single picture from the woods.

"That can't be!" you exclaim.

The officers suggest you return to your hotel and get some rest. "No offense, but this place can be a lot to take in for city folks," one of them says.

You explain to Clara that you have to leave the next day. She promises you can reconnect another time and drives you back to your hotel.

You leave Fairbanks in the morning still
not feeling entirely well and with unanswered
questions about that night in the woods.

THE END

To read another, turn to page 17.
To learn more about aliens, turn to page 106.

Your heart is pounding so hard you wonder if anyone else could hear it. You snap a few pictures then sneak closer to get a better vantage point. As you do so, you trip over rock and yelp. The figures turn toward your direction.

Your headache gets sharper and there's a ringing in your ears. You feel like you're floating seemingly out of your body. You cling onto the rock, but your grip is slipping as though an unseen force is pulling you away from it by your legs.

Panic sets in.

You lose your hold on the rock and fall to the ground. You dig your nails in the dirt and leaves but you continue to be pulled away. You open your mouth to scream, but no sound comes out. Maybe you did scream but you couldn't hear it from the ringing in your ears.

Victims of supposed alien abductions often describe being lifted into a spacecraft by a beam of light.

Turn the page.

The next day, Clara, Roscoe, and two police officers comb through the woods looking for you. When Clara returned the night before and couldn't find you, she called the police. Now she is calling out your name.

Roscoe trots beside her sniffing the ground as he goes along. He stops abruptly at the rock you were hiding behind and barks. Clara and the officers run toward Roscoe.

They find your cell phone and camera among a pile of leaves. The screen on the phone is cracked and neither it nor the camera would turn on. Roscoe whines. The group continues to search the woods but finds no sign of you.

"I'm sorry," one of the officers tells Clara.

"No one can just disappear into thin air," Clara says. She pauses and then looks up at the sky. "Can they?"

THE END

To read another, turn to page 17.
To learn more about aliens, turn to page 106.

A large radio telescope dish at the Arecibo Observatory in Barrio Esperanza, Arecibo, Puerto Rico

CHAPTER 5

CONCLUSION

Some say if aliens are visiting us, maybe we should communicate with them. On November 16, 1974, the Arecibo Observatory telescope in Puerto Rico was used to send the most powerful broadcast ever sent into space to contact alien life.

Designed by scientists, the broadcast consisted of a pattern of binary numbers—ones and zeros. This message contained information about the basic chemicals of life, the structure of DNA, Earth's place in our solar system, and a stick figure of a human.

Turn the page.

According to the Search for Extraterrestrial Intelligence Institute in California, which has a telescope array to search for alien life, "The experiment was useful in getting us to think a bit about the difficulties of communicating across space, time, and a presumably wide culture gap." Some people praise these attempts to communicate with extraterrestrial life while others fear it is not safe considering it is not known who will respond. The world is still waiting for a reply.

In 1977, NASA launched *Voyager 1* and *Voyager 2*. These spacecraft carry identical 12-inch, gold-plated phonograph records along with instructions on how to play them. The records contain images, including a map of our solar system, male and female bodies, snowflakes, trees, dolphins, and a supermarket.

NASA's *Voyager 1* space probe

Turn the page.

The records also included sounds, such as wind, thunder, bird and whale calls, music from various cultures, and greetings in 55 languages. However, the spacecraft won't approach another star for at least 40,000 years.

In the meantime, scientists have found planets that may hold alien life. Planets that orbit around stars other than the sun are called exoplanets. More than 4,000 exoplanets are confirmed to exist in our galaxy. But there are likely trillions.

These exoplanets may have conditions that could allow for the existence of some form of life. Could these exoplanets be the home of alien beings, and have they visited Earth? Are they soaring through our skies in their spacecraft right now observing, studying, and learning about us?

The Hubble Ultra Deep Field 2014, an image created using Hubble Space Telescope data, features nearly 10,000 galaxies in a small area of sky.

Turn the page.

Are they hidden in a top-secret facility? Are they taking humans on their spacecraft? Do they intend to protect humans? Or do they have other plans?

The search for the truth continues.

More Aliens and Extraterrestrials

Based on descriptions provided by individuals who have reportedly seen aliens, there are different types of beings that visit, or have visited, Earth.

Greys

This is the most common type of reported aliens. Greys have a body shape similar to humans. They are grey-skinned, 3 feet (1 meter) tall, hairless, and have large heads and black eyes. They are said to have small noses, slits for mouths, tiny or possibly no ears, and three to four fingers. Some say they can read minds, communicate telepathically, and even shapeshift into different lifeforms, including humans.

Nordic Aliens or Tall Whites

They are described as tall humanoids with blonde hair and blue eyes.

Reptilians

Described as tall, scaly humanoids, they are said to be beings sighted back at least as far as Ancient Egypt.

Hopkinsville Goblin

These small, greenish-silver humanoids were part of a claimed close encounter with extraterrestrials in 1955 near Kelly and Hopkinsville in Kentucky. Skeptics say the reports were due to "the effects of excitement" and misidentification of natural phenomena such as meteors and owls.

Glossary

alleged (uh-LEJ-uhd)—said to have taken place but not proven

credentials (krih-DEN-shulz)—documents showing that a person has a right to perform certain official acts

debunk (dee-BUHNK)—to expose as being false or exaggerated

declassify (dee-KLAS-ih-fye)—officially declare to be no longer secret

encounter (in-KOWNT-ur)—to come upon face-to-face, or meet

enthusiast (en-THOO-zee-uhst)—a person who is interested in a particular activity or subject

exoplanet (EKS-oh-plah-net)—a planet that orbits a star outside our solar system

extraterrestrial (eks-truh-ter-RESS-tree-uhl)—outside or beyond the earth

eyewitness (aye-WIT-ness)—a person who sees an occurrence and is able to give a report of it

hearsay (HEER-say)—information that can't be proven, or a rumor

hoax (HOHKS)—falsehood disguised as truth

installation (in-stuh-LAY-shuhn)—a military base

phenomenon (fi-NAHM-ih-nahn)—an exceptional, unusual, or abnormal person or thing

photoshop (FOH-toh-shawp)—to alter a digital image with Photoshop software or other image-editing software

physicist (FIZ-ih-sist)—a scientist who studies physics, the science of nature and properties of matter and energy

task force (TASK FORS)—a group specially organized for a task

unclassified (uhn-KLAS-ih-fyed)—not secret and is available to the public

Other Paths to Explore

>>> Men in Black—In the story, the reporter
repeatedly encounters two strange men. Could
they be the infamous Men in Black? In popular
culture and conspiracy theories, the Men in Black
usually dress in black suits. Some believe they also
disguise themselves. They are said to harass or
threaten UFO researchers and witnesses to stop
them from talking about what they have seen.
They are allegedly tasked with protecting secrets.

>>> Exoplanets—Planets that orbit around stars other
than the sun are called exoplanets. More than
4,000 exoplanets are confirmed to exist in our
galaxy. But there are likely trillions. According to
scientists, life on an exoplanet is possible if liquid
water could exist on the planet.

>>> Interstellar Message—In 1974, scientists used a
giant radio telescope at the Arecibo Observatory
in Puerto Rico to send a radio broadcast into outer
space. The message contained information about
the basic chemicals of life, the structure of DNA,
Earth's place in our solar system, and a stick figure
of a human. Earth has yet to receive a response.

Read More

Kim, Carol. *Area 51 Alien and UFO Mysteries*. North Mankato, MN: Capstone, 2021.

Kenney, Karen Latchana. *Mysterious UFOs and Aliens*. Minneapolis: Lerner Publications, 2018.

Webb, Stuart. *Paranormal Files: UFOs*. New York: Rosen Publishing, 2013.

Internet Sites

TKSST: Are There Aliens Out There?
thekidshouldseethis.com/post/are-there-aliens-royal-observatory-greenwich-investigates

NASA: Aliens Among Us?
nasa.gov/audience/foreducators/informal/features/F_Aliens_Among_Us.html

Britannica Kids: Extraterrestrial Life
kids.britannica.com/students/article/extraterrestrial-life/274243

About the Author

Cristina Oxtra is the author of *Tara and the Towering Wave: An Indian Ocean Tsunami Survival Story* and the graphic novel *Red Riding Hood*. She earned an MFA in creative writing for children and young adults from Hamline University. Cristina lives in Minnesota, where she enjoys cooking, baking, martial arts, and exploring the paranormal.

Other Books in This Series

YOU CHOOSE

CAN YOU TRACK DOWN BIGFOOT?

41 CHOICES
20 ENDINGS

BY BRAN

YOU CHOOSE

CAN YOU NET THE LOCH NESS MONSTER?

49 CHOICES
21 ENDINGS

BY BRANDON TERRELL AND MATT DOEDEN

YOU CHOOSE

CAN YOU CATCH THE KRAKEN?

41 CHOICES
21 ENDINGS

BY BRANDON TERRELL

YOU CHOOSE

CAN YOU CAPTURE THE CHUPACABRA?

37 CHOICES
16 ENDINGS

BY BRANDON TERRELL AND BLAKE HOENA